The Canterville Ghost

from the story by
Oscar Wilde

Adapted by Susanna Davidson

Illustrated by
Alan Marks

Reading Consultant: Alison Kelly
University of Surrey Roehampton

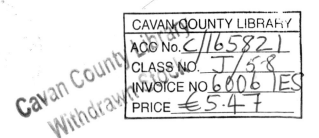

Contents

Chapter 1

Canterville Castle

Canterville Castle
FOR SALE

Mr. Otis looked at the castle with delight. "I'll buy it!" he cried.

"Excellent," replied his guide, Lord Canterville. "But perhaps I should warn you... Canterville Castle is haunted."

3

"My family had to move out many years ago, after my great-aunt had a dreadful experience."

"She never recovered."

Mr. Otis wasn't worried. He didn't believe in ghosts.

A week later, Mr. and Mrs. Otis arrived with their children, Washington, Virginia and the twins. They were greeted by an old woman, who was neatly dressed in a white apron and cap.

Welcome to Canterville Castle.

"I'm Mrs. Umney, the housekeeper," she said. "Come inside. There's tea for you in the library."

"Cake!" shouted the twins, diving in. Virginia wasn't interested in the food. She had spotted a poem in the library window.

Before she could show her father, Mrs. Otis cried out. "Oh dear! I'm afraid we've spilled something on the carpet, Mrs. Umney."

"It wasn't you madam," replied Mrs. Umney in a hushed voice. "*Blood* has been spilled there."

"How horrible!" cried Mrs. Otis. "It must be removed at once."

Mrs. Umney looked around nervously and began to speak in a low voice.

"It is the blood of Lady Eleanor Canterville. She was murdered on that very spot by her husband, Sir Simon Canterville, five hundred years ago."

Oh dear!

"Seven years later, Sir Simon Canterville disappeared. His body has never been found."

Mrs. Umney's voice began to shake. "His spirit haunts this house. That blood stain will never go."

Washington jumped down onto the carpet and scrubbed at the blood stain. Within seconds, it was gone.

But as he stood up there was a
crash of thunder and a terrible
flash of lightning.

Mrs. Umney fainted.

The thunderstorm lasted the
entire night. Rain lashed at the
windows and the wind howled
down the chimneys.

And next morning, in the very same spot on the library carpet, there was the blood stain.

Chapter 2

Clanking chains

"There must be a simple explanation," cried Mr. Otis.

That night, Mr. Otis locked the library door himself and took the key to bed with him. But the blood stain still came back.

After what happened the following night, Mr. Otis thought differently about ghosts.

At midnight, he was woken by
a strange noise outside his room.
It sounded like rusty chains being
dragged along the ground and it
seemed to be coming closer
every second.

What's that noise?

Mr. Otis was annoyed. He put on
his slippers and picked up a small
bottle from his bedside table. Then
he opened the door...

...to a terrible sight. An old man, with long greasy hair and ragged clothes was glaring at him out of fiery red eyes.

"You must be Sir Simon," said Mr. Otis calmly. "I'm afraid, my dear sir, I must ask you to oil your chains. They make an awful noise. This bottle of oil should help."

Mr. Otis left the bottle on a table and went back to bed.

For a moment the Canterville
Ghost was still. Then
he smashed the
bottle of oil onto
the floor and
fled down the
corridor,
howling.

Whooooooooh!

18

The twins heard him. As Sir
Simon reached the top of the stairs,
they raced out of their bedroom
with a pillow. Sir Simon felt a rush
of air as the pillow whizzed past
his head. It very nearly hit him.

The ghost quickly vanished, to appear in his secret chamber in the west wing. He was furious. "I have been scaring people for hundreds of years," he grumbled, "but never have I been treated like this."

They should have been terrified!

"How dare these newcomers give me oil for my chains and throw pillows at my head. I must get my revenge!"

Chapter 3

The ghost's revenge

"There's no
need to be scared
of ghosts," Mr. Otis told his family
the next morning, "but you mustn't
throw pillows at them. It's rude."

The twins grinned.

"We'll have to take those chains off him," said Mrs. Otis, "or we'll never get any sleep." But for the rest of that week there was no sign of the ghost.

The twins looked for him everywhere. They wanted to play more tricks on him.

Fresh blood stains continued to appear each morning. Strangely, each stain was a different shade. The family made guesses as to what shade it would be next.

One morning, it was even a brilliant green. When she saw that, Virginia looked cross, though she wouldn't say why.

Meanwhile, the ghost was busy plotting his revenge. He spent days looking over his wardrobe, deciding what to wear.

Perfect! The ripped sheet and the rusty dagger.

He planned to creep to Washington's room and make faces at the boy from the foot of his bed. Then, he would stab himself in the neck three times to the sound of slow music.

Sir Simon especially disliked Washington. It was Washington who kept removing the blood stains.

Virginia, on the other hand, had never been rude. "I shall only groan at her a few times from her wardrobe," he thought. "As for the twins..."

The twins, of course, deserved the worst treatment. He'd get them. He would turn into a skeleton and crawl around their beds, staring at them from one rolling eyeball.

At half-past ten the family went
to bed. For a while Sir Simon heard
shrieks of laughter from the twins'
room, but at last all was quiet.

He crept stealthily into the
corridor. An owl beat its wings
against the window pane, but
the Otis family slept on,
peacefully unaware.

Sir Simon glided along like an evil shadow, a cruel smile stretching his wrinkled mouth. Finally, he reached the corner of the passage that led to Washington's room.

Ha ha! The time has come.

He chuckled to himself, turned the corner, then let out a wail of terror. Sir Simon fell back, hiding his face in his bony white hands.

Right in front of him was a
horrible vision. It was bald and
white, with red light
streaming from its eyes. Sir
Simon had never seen
another ghost before.
He was terrified.

Aaargh!

He fled back to his room,
tripping on his sheet as he went.

Back in his chamber, he flung himself into his coffin and slammed down the lid. But as the sun rose, his bravery returned.

"I shall go and talk to the ghost," he decided. "Perhaps we can deal with the twins together."

Two ghosts are better than one.

By morning the ghost looked very different. The light had gone from its eyes and it had collapsed against the wall.

Sir Simon rushed forward and seized it in his arms. To his horror, its head slipped off and rolled on the floor.

What's happened?

He was holding a white curtain, a broom and a large pumpkin. He had been tricked! Sir Simon ground his toothless gums together in fury, swore revenge and stomped back to his coffin.

Chapter 4

Sir Simon is upset

Sir Simon was cross and tired. The excitement of the past few days had been too much for him. For five days he stayed in his room. He even gave up making new blood stains.

What's the point? They don't take me seriously.

With the twins constantly playing tricks on him, he only felt safe in his room. He knew it was his ghostly duty to appear in the corridor once a week, but he made sure he wasn't seen or heard.

He even slipped into Mr. Otis's bedroom and took a bottle of oil for his chains. But he still wasn't left alone.

The twins put down pins for him to tread on. One night they even stretched a piece of string across the corridor.

"That's it!" he decided. "I'm going to scare those twins one last time, if it kills me."

"I'll appear as my most terrifying character, Reckless Rupert the Headless Earl," he thought. Reckless Rupert always worked.

Not bad. Not bad at all.

Sir Simon spent two days getting ready. Finally, he was satisfied with his appearance.

As the clock struck midnight, he made his way to the twins' bedroom. He flung open the door...

...and a large jug of icy water tipped over him. He was soaked. Sir Simon heard muffled shrieks of laughter from the twins' beds.

Furious, Sir Simon squelched back to his room. The next day he had a very bad cold. "I must give up all hope of scaring the Otis family," he said sadly.

Why aren't I scary anymore? Perhaps I'm getting old.

He started creeping along the passages in his slippers.

One night he decided to creep to
the library. He wanted to see if there
was any blood left on the carpet.
Suddenly, two figures jumped out at
him from the darkness.

In terror, Sir Simon
ran to the stairs. But
there was
Washington Otis,
aiming a garden
hose at him.

Sir Simon vanished into the fireplace, which – luckily for him – wasn't lit. He arrived back in his room in a terrible state.

Look at me! I'm covered in soot!

After that, he did not leave his room at all. The Otis family started to think the ghost had left.

The twins lay in wait for Sir Simon for several nights, but there was no sign of him.

"I'll write a letter to Lord Canterville," said Mr. Otis. "I'm sure he'll be interested to hear that Sir Simon has gone away at last."

Chapter 5

The secret chamber

Some weeks later, Virginia was out walking in the fields, when she tore her dress climbing through a hedge.

Oh no! Mama will be furious.

"I'll have to change," she thought, and decided to go up the back staircase, so she wouldn't be seen. On the way, she noticed that the door to the Tapestry Room was open.

"How odd!" she thought. "No one ever uses the Tapestry Room." Virginia peered around the door. To her surprise, she saw the Canterville Ghost.

Sir Simon was sitting by the window, his head in his hands. He looked so upset Virginia thought she should try and comfort him.

We thought you'd gone!

"Cheer up," she said. "The boys
are going to school tomorrow, so
the tricks will stop.
Besides, if you behave
yourself, no one will
annoy you."

You don't
understand!

Sir Simon jumped up. "How can
I behave myself?" he shouted. "I
have to rattle my chains and groan
through keyholes and walk around
at night. I'm a ghost."

43

"You don't *have* to do anything," said Virginia. "What's more, you've been very wicked. Mrs. Umney told us that you murdered your wife. It's wrong to kill people," she pointed out.

Very wrong indeed.

"Yes, it was wrong," sighed Sir Simon, "but that was no reason for her brothers to starve me to death."

"Oh, poor ghost!" said Virginia.
"I didn't know about that. Are you
hungry now?"

Perhaps you'd like some sandwiches?

"No thank you," he answered.
"I never eat now. But it's kind of
you to offer. You know," he added,
"you're much nicer than the rest
of your horrible family."

"How dare you be rude about my family!" cried Virginia. "You're mean, you lie *and* you stole all the paints out of my paint box for that blood stain. First my reds, then the yellows – even the greens."

I couldn't paint anything.

"I think you should apologize," Virginia demanded.

The ghost shrugged. "I don't see why I should. After all, what else could I do? Real blood is so hard to get hold of these days. And your brother would keep cleaning up."

"Fine," said Virginia. "If you won't apologize, I'm leaving." She turned to go.

No! Please don't go!

"Please help me," Sir Simon called. "I'm so unhappy and so very, very tired."

Now Virginia was curious. "Why are you tired?"

"I haven't slept for five hundred years," Sir Simon told her.

Virginia gasped.

"And it would be so pleasant to lie in the soft brown earth," the ghost went on, "with grasses waving above my head, listening to silence..."

"Can't anyone help you?" asked Virginia.

"You could," whispered the ghost.

Virginia trembled as he spoke and a cold shudder passed through her. "How?" she asked.

"Have you ever read the poem on the library window?"

"Yes, often." Virginia thought of it now.

If a child will enter the secret room

And stay till the dead of the night

Then at last Sir Simon can sleep in his tomb

And at Canterville all will be right.

"But I don't know what it means."

"It means," said the ghost, "that you must come with me to my secret chamber and pray for me."

"That sounds easy," said Virginia.

"Mmm," said Sir Simon, "but no living person has ever entered the chamber and come out alive."

Virginia was terrified. But she did want to help. "I'll come with you Sir Simon," she said bravely. "Lead the way."

Sir Simon took her hand in his cold, clammy fingers. Together they walked to the end of the room, where the wall disappeared before her eyes.

In a moment, the wall had closed behind them and Virginia vanished into the ghost's secret chamber.

Chapter 6

Peace at last

Ten minutes later the bell rang for tea. As Virginia did not appear, Mrs. Otis sent a footman to find her.

I can't find her anywhere, ma'am.

At first Mrs. Otis thought she must be in the stables. When Virginia still hadn't returned two hours later, she began to panic.

"Boys," she called to her sons, "go and see if you can find her."

She's vanished!

Oh! Where can she be?

Mrs. Otis even asked Mr. Otis to drain the fish pond. But there was no sign of Virginia anywhere.

At last the family sat down to supper. It was a sad meal and hardly anyone spoke. Even the twins were quiet. As the family left the dining room, the clock in the tower began to strike midnight.

On the last stroke there was a crash and a sudden, shrill cry. A panel at the top of the staircase flew back and Virginia staggered out.

Everyone rushed up to her. Mrs. Otis hugged her, Mr. Otis patted her head and the twins danced around them all.

"Where have you been?" said Mrs. Otis, rather angrily.

I've been so worried. You must not play tricks Virginia.

Except on the ghost!

56

"I've been with the ghost," said
Virginia quietly. "He's gone. He's
been very wicked, but he was sorry
for everything he'd done. And look!
He gave me this box of jewels just
before he left."

Four days later, they held a funeral for Sir Simon. The procession left Canterville Castle at eleven o'clock at night. The carriages were drawn by four black horses, each with a great tuft of ostrich-feathers on its head.

Don't you think 500 years is rather long to wait for a funeral?

Lord Canterville came all the way from Wales to take part. He sat in the first carriage with Virginia. Then came Mr. and Mrs. Otis, followed by Washington and the twins.

It was all wonderfully impressive.

In the last carriage sat Mrs. Umney. After all, she had been frightened of the ghost for fifty years. It was only fair she should see the last of him.

The next day Mr. Otis had a word with Lord Canterville. "I think we should return the box of jewels to you. They're beautiful. Especially the ruby necklace."

Please take them.

"No thank you, Mr. Otis," replied Lord Canterville. "The jewels were given to Virginia for being so brave and I think she deserves them."

Virginia wore the ruby necklace whenever she went to a party. But, however much Washington and the twins begged, she never told anyone what happened in the secret chamber.

Z
Z
z
z

Sir Simon
Canterville
R.I.P.

Oscar Wilde
1854-1900

The writer Oscar Wilde was born in
Ireland, but moved to London when he
was 24. His first book, *Poems*, was
published in 1881. *The Canterville
Ghost* was written in
1887. Wilde also
wrote fairy tales
for his two sons,
but he is best
known for his
plays, which are
still performed
today.

Series editor: Lesley Sims

Designed by
Russell Punter

First published in 2004 by Usborne Publishing Ltd., Usborne House,
83-85 Saffron Hill, London EC1N 8RT, England. www.usborne.com
Copyright © 2004 Usborne Publishing Ltd.